ANNA SEWELL'S

BLACK BEAUTY

THE GRAPHIC NOVEL

adapted by **June Brigman & Roy Richardson**

PUFFIN BOOKS

Visit us at www.abdopub.com

Spotlight, a division of ABDO Publishing Company, is a distributor of high quality reinforced library bound editions for schools and libraries.

This library bound edition is published by arrangement with Penguin Young Readers Group, a member of Penguin Group (USA) Inc.

Library of Congress Cataloging-In-Publication Data

PUFFIN BOOKS
Published by the Penguin Group
Penguin Young Readers Group,
345 Hudson Street, New York, NY 10014 U.S.A.

Black Beauty Graphic Novel first published by Puffin Books, a division of Penguin Young Readers Group, 2005

A Byron Preiss Book
Byron Preiss Visual Publications
24 West 25th Street, New York, NY 10010

Art assistants: Bob Berry, Al Milgrom and Keith Williams
Special thanks to Michael Kaluta for reference and inspiration.
Cover art by Bob Larkin
Lettering by J. Vita
Series Editor: Dwight Jon Zimmerman
Series Assistant Editor: April Isaacs
Interior design by M. Postawa and Gilda Hannah
Cover design by M. Postawa

Puffin Books ISBN 0-14-240408-X
ISBN: 1-59961-113-9 Reinforced Library Bound Edition

All Spotlight books are reinforced library binding and manufactured in the United States of America.

BLACK BEAUTY

CHAPTER ONE: MY EARLY HOME

MEN CALL ME **BLACK BEAUTY**.
THIS IS MY STORY.

THE **FIRST PLACE** THAT I CAN WELL
REMEMBER WAS A LARGE PLEASANT
MEADOW WITH A POND OF CLEAR
WATER ON IT.

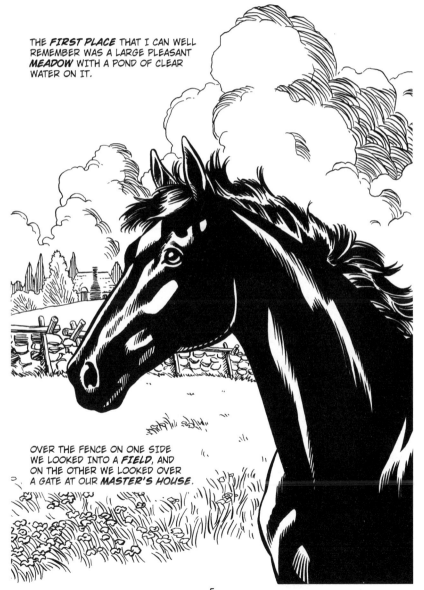

OVER THE FENCE ON ONE SIDE
WE LOOKED INTO A **FIELD**, AND
ON THE OTHER WE LOOKED OVER
A GATE AT OUR **MASTER'S HOUSE**.

AS SOON AS I WAS OLD ENOUGH TO EAT GRASS, MY **MOTHER** USED TO GO OUT TO **WORK** IN THE DAYTIME, AND COME BACK IN THE EVENING.

THERE WERE SIX YOUNG **COLTS** IN THE **MEADOW** BESIDE ME. I USED TO RUN WITH THEM, AND WE HAD **GREAT FUN**.

WE HAD RATHER **ROUGH PLAY**, FOR THEY WOULD FREQUENTLY BITE AND KICK.

ONE DAY MY MOTHER SAID TO ME, "THE COLTS WHO LIVE HERE ARE VERY **GOOD COLTS** BUT THEY HAVE NOT LEARNED **MANNERS**. I HOPE YOU WILL GROW UP GENTLE AND GOOD AND NEVER BITE OR KICK EVEN IN **PLAY**."

MY MOTHER WAS A **WISE OLD HORSE**, AND I HAVE NEVER FORGOTTEN HER ADVICE.

6

7

CHAPTER 2: THE HUNT

ONE DAY IN THE **SPRING** SOMETHING OCCURRED WHICH I HAVE NEVER FORGOTTEN.

"IT IS THE **HUNT!**" SAID THE OLDEST OF THE COLTS.

"LOOK! THEY HAVE FOUND A **HARE!**" SAID MY MOTHER.

A **SAD SIGHT**, TWO FINE HORSES DOWN, AND THE RIDER ISN'T MOVING.

"HIS NECK IS **BROKEN**," SAID MY MOTHER.

I HEARD AFTERWARDS THAT IT WAS YOUNG **GEORGE GORDON**, THE SQUIRE'S ONLY SON.

8

ONE OF THE FALLEN HORSES HAD A **BROKEN LEG**. SOMEONE RAN TO OUR MASTER'S HOUSE AND CAME BACK WITH A GUN. THERE WAS A **LOUD BANG**...

THE BLACK HORSE MOVED **NO MORE**.

MY MOTHER SEEMED MUCH **TROUBLED**; SHE SAID SHE HAD KNOWN THAT HORSE FOR YEARS, AND THAT HIS NAME WAS **"ROB ROY."** HE WAS A GOOD BOLD HORSE, AND THERE WAS NO VICE IN HIM. SHE NEVER WOULD GO TO THAT PART OF THE **FIELD** AFTERWARDS.

NOT MANY DAYS AFTER WE SAW A LONG STRANGE **BLACK COACH** THAT WAS COVERED WITH BLACK CLOTH AND WAS DRAWN BY **BLACK HORSES**.

THEY WERE CARRYING YOUNG GORDON TO THE **CHURCHYARD** TO **BURY** HIM. WHAT THEY DID WITH ROB ROY I NEVER KNEW, BUT 'TWAS ALL FOR ONE LITTLE HARE.

9

CHAPTER 3: MY BREAKING IN

BY AGE **FOUR** MY **MASTER** DECIDED IT WAS TIME TO **SELL** ME. **SQUIRE GORDON** CAME TO LOOK AT ME.

WHEN HE HAS BEEN **BROKEN IN**, HE WILL DO VERY WELL.

MY MASTER SAID HE WOULD **BREAK ME IN** HIMSELF, BEGINNING THE VERY NEXT DAY.

BREAKING IN MEANS TO **TEACH** A HORSE TO WEAR A SADDLE AND BRIDLE, **CARRY** A MAN ON HIS BACK, WEAR A **HARNESS** AND PULL A CART. WORST OF ALL, HE MUST **LEARN** TO ALWAYS DO HIS MASTER'S WILL.

I WAS **FITTED** WITH A NASTY BIT, A **TRAINING SADDLE**, AND HEAVY IRON SHOES.

IT WAS VERY **STRANGE**, BUT I GOT USED TO IT, AND LEARNED TO DO MY JOB.

AS PART OF MY *TRAINING* I WAS SENT TO A MEADOW THAT SKIRTED A *RAILWAY*. I SHALL NEVER FORGET THE FIRST *TRAIN* THAT WENT BY.

I GALLOPED TO THE *FAR SIDE* OF THE MEADOW, SNORTING WITH ASTONISHMENT AND *FEAR*.

AFTER A FEW DAYS I BEGAN TO *IGNORE* IT. THUS WAS I TRAINED NOT TO BE FEARFUL AT *RAILWAY STATIONS*.

MY MOTHER TOLD ME THE *BETTER* I BEHAVED, THE BETTER MY *LIFE* WOULD BE. SHE SAID:

"THERE ARE MANY KINDS OF MEN, GOOD AND BAD, AND YOU NEVER KNOW WHO WILL BUY YOU. DO YOUR BEST AND KEEP YOUR GOOD NAME."

CHAPTER FOUR: BIRTWICK PARK

IN EARLY **MAY**, A MAN CAME TO TAKE ME TO SQUIRE GORDON'S.

GOODBYE, BLACKIE. BE A *GOOD HORSE*, AND ALWAYS DO YOUR BEST.

SO I SAID **FAREWELL** TO THE ONLY HOME I HAD EVER KNOWN.

SQUIRE GORDON'S PARK WAS NEAR THE VILLAGE OF **BIRTWICK**. IT WAS A LARGE ESTATE, WITH **MEADOWS**, TREES, AND **FINE GARDENS**.

I WAS TAKEN TO A ROOMY **STABLE** WITH FOUR GOOD **STALLS**. IT WAS AIRY AND PLEASANT.

I WAS PUT INTO A NICE LARGE **STALL**, AND LEFT UNTIED. I ATE SOME OATS AND LOOKED AROUND AT MY **NEW NEIGHBORS**.

"HELLO, MY NAME IS **MERRYLEGS**. I'M A HANDSOME PONY, AND I CARRY THE **YOUNG LADIES** ON MY BACK. ARE YOU MY NEW STALL MATE?"

"SO THIS IS THE YOUNG **UPSTART** WHO HAS TAKEN MY NICE LARGE STALL. IT IS A **STRANGE THING** FOR A COLT LIKE YOU TO TURN A LADY OUT OF HER HOME!"

"DON'T MIND HER, THAT'S **GINGER**. SHE WAS MOVED BECAUSE SHE BIT ONE OF THE **GROOMS**, SO YOU SEE IT'S NOT YOUR FAULT. IT IS VERY **NICE** HERE IF YOU DON'T BITE OR SNAP."

CHAPTER 5: A FAIR START

THE NEXT MORNING THE **COACHMAN JOHN MANLY** TOOK ME INTO THE YARD FOR A GOOD **GROOMING**. THE SQUIRE CAME TO LOOK ME OVER.

I MEANT TO **TRY** THIS ONE OUT MYSELF, BUT I HAVE OTHER BUSINESS THIS **MORNING**. YOU TAKE ROUND THIS MORNING. LET HIM SHOW HIS PACES.

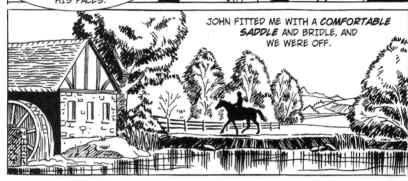

JOHN FITTED ME WITH A **COMFORTABLE SADDLE** AND BRIDLE, AND WE WERE OFF.

WHEN WE CAME TO AN **OPEN FIELD** HE GAVE ME A LIGHT TOUCH WITH HIS **WHIP**, AND WE HAD A **SPLENDID GALLOP**.

HOHO, MY BOY!

YOU WOULD LIKE TO FOLLOW THE **HOUNDS**, I THINK.

AS WE CAME BACK, WE MET THE SQUIRE AND HIS *WIFE* WALKING.

WELL, JOHN, HOW DOES HE *GO*?

FIRST RATE, SIR. HE IS AS FLEET AS A DEER, AND HAS A *FINE SPIRIT*, TOO.

THAT'S WELL. I WILL TRY HIM MYSELF *TOMORROW*.

WE SET OFF EARLY THE *NEXT MORNING*. THE SQUIRE WAS A VERY *GOOD RIDER*, AND THOUGHTFUL FOR HIS HORSE, TOO.

HE IS *EVERY BIT* THE HORSE JOHN SAID HE WAS. WHAT SHALL WE *CALL* HIM, MY DEAR?

FOR SUCH A FINE HORSE, I THINK ONLY *"BLACK BEAUTY"* WILL DO.

BLACK BEAUTY IT SHALL BE THEN!

15

JOHN MANLY AND JAMES THE STABLE BOY APROVED OF MY NEW NAME.

A SENSIBLE *ENGLISH NAME*, NOT LIKE PEGASUS, OR SOME SUCH.

THE NEXT DAY I HAD TO PULL THE *CARRIAGE* WITH GINGER. I WONDERED HOW WE WOULD GET ON TOGETHER.

SHE BEHAVED *VERY WELL*, AND DID HER FULL SHARE OF WORK. WE BECAME *FRIENDS* AFTER ALL.

AS FOR MERRYLEGS, HE AND I SOON BECAME *GREAT FRIENDS.* HE WAS A FAVORITE WITH EVERYONE.

...ESPECIALLY THE *SQUIRE'S DAUGHTER.*

THE SQUIRE HAD *TWO OTHER HORSES* THAT LIVED IN ANOTHER STABLE. *JUSTICE* WAS A ROAN COB. THE OTHER WAS *SIR OLIVER,* A RETIRED HUNTER WHO WAS A FORVORITE OF THE MASTER.

WE GOT ON, BUT I WAS NOT AS *CLOSE* TO THEM AS I WAS TO MY STABLEMATE, GINGER.

CHAPTER 6: LIBERTY

I WAS QUITE **HAPPY** IN MY NEW PLACE. ALL WHO HAD TO DO WITH ME WERE GOOD, AND I HAD A LIGHT, AIRY STABLE AND THE BEST OF FOOD. WHAT MORE COULD WANT? WHY, I **LIBERTY!**

SOMETIMES, IT WAS **TOO MUCH**, AND I COULD NOT KEEP QUIET. I HAD TO JUMP, TO PRANCE, TO FEEL **FREE!**

STEADY, MY BOY, STEADY!

OUR JOHN UNDERSTOOD. HE WAS QUITE **PATIENT**, AND I WAS VERY FOND OF HIM.

I OUGHT TO SAY THAT **SOMETIMES** WE DID HAVE OUR LIBERTY FOR A FEW HOURS. THIS WAS ON FINE SUNDAYS IN THE **SUMMERTIME.**

THIS WAS A VERY GOOD TIME FOR **TALKING**, AS WE STOOD TOGETHER UNDER THE SHADE OF THE HUGE **CHESTNUT TREE.**

CHAPTER 7: GINGER

ONE SUNDAY GINGER ASKED ABOUT MY *UPBRINGING*, AND I TOLD HER.

"WELL," SAID SHE, "IF I HAD HAD YOUR BRINGING UP, I MIGHT HAVE BEEN OF AS *GOOD TEMPERED* AS YOU ARE, BUT NOW I DON'T BELIEVE I EVER SHALL."

"WHY NOT?" I SAID.

"BECAUSE I *NEVER* HAD ANY ONE, HORSE OR MAN, THAT WAS *KIND* TO ME. BOYS PELTED ME WITH *STONES* FOR FUN.

"WHEN IT WAS TIME FOR BREAKING IN, IT WAS VERY *BAD* FOR ME. SEVERAL MEN SEIZED ME CRUELLY, AND FORCED A HALTER ON ME. MY *BREAKERS* KNEW NOTHING OF GENTLENESS, ONLY *FORCE* AND ROUGHNESS."

"THE **SON** OF THE MASTER WAS THE **HEAD BREAKER.** HIS NAME WAS SAMSON, AND THERE WAS NO KINDNESS IN HIM AT ALL, ONLY **HARDNESS** AND CRUELTY."

"HIS ONE THOUGHT WAS TO TURN ME INTO AN OBEDIENT PIECE OF **HUMBLED HORSEFLESH!**"

"ONE DAY HE WORKED ME VERY HARD TO TIRE ME OUT, TO **BREAK MY SPIRIT**."

"THEN HE MOUNTED ME AND BEGAN TO **BEAT ME** WITH A WHIP."

"I KICKED AND REARED. AFTER A **TERRIBLE STRUGGLE**, I THREW HIM OFF BACKWARDS."

"HE ROSE AND LEFT ME STANDING IN THE **HOT SUN**, THIRSTY AND BLEEDING FROM HIS HEAVY WHIP."

"AFTER MY BREAKING IN, I WAS **SOLD** TO A FASHIONABLE GENTLEMAN FROM LONDON.

"HE USED A **CRUEL BEARING REIN** ON US TO HOLD OUR HEADS HIGH, TO MAKE US LOOK MORE **STYLISH.** IT IS A DREADFUL, PAINFUL DEVICE, AND I GREW TO HATE IT.

"ONE DAY THEY BUCKLED US IN PARTICULARLY **TIGHT,** AND I COULD TAKE IT NO LONGER. I KICKED AND BUCKED UNTIL I WAS **FREE,** AND THAT WAS THE END OF THAT PLACE."

"I WAS **SOLD** TO A COUNTRY GENTLEMAN WHO DROVE ME WITHOUT A BEARING REIN, AND SO FOR A WHILE I GOT ON VERY WELL.

"BUT THEN HIS KIND OLD GROOM LEFT HIM, AND A **NEW ONE** CAME.

"THIS MAN WAS AS HARD AND **CRUEL** AS SAMSON. ANY LITTLE THING I DID TO DISPLEASE HIM WAS MET WITH A BLOW FROM HIS **PITCHFORK.** I QUICKLY LEARNED TO HATE HIM.

"ONE DAY HE PUSHED ME TOO FAR, AND I **BIT** HIM. THIS OF COURSE THREW HIM INTO A GREAT RAGE.

"HE BEAT ME SEVERELY WITH A **RIDING WHIP.** HE TOLD THE MASTER I WAS **DANGEROUS**, AND SO I WAS SOLD AGAIN."

"AFTER ALL I HAVE BEEN THROUGH, I HAVE *LITTLE TRUST* IN MEN."

I WAS *SORRY* FOR GINGER, BUT KNEW LITTLE THEN, AND THOUGHT SHE HAD MADE THE WORSE OF HER *TALE.*

AS THE WEEKS WENT ON, SHE GREW MUCH MORE *GENTLE* AND CHEERFUL, AND LOST HER DEFIANT LOOK. EVEN THE MASTER *NOTICED.*

WELL, MY PRETTY ONE, YOU ARE A GOOD BIT *HAPPIER* THAN WHEN YOU CAME TO US, I THINK.

YES SIR, SHE'S WONDER-FULLY IMPROVED. ALL SHE WANTED WAS A LITTLE *KINDNESS*, POOR THING.

CHAPTER 9: MERRYLEGS

THERE, YOU *ROGUE*, MIND HOW YOU BEHAVE YOURSELF, OR WE SHALL GET INTO TROUBLE!

ONE AFTERNOON, AN *ANGRY* JAMES BROUGHT BACK MERRYLEGS, WHO HAD BEEN OUT A LONG TIME WITH A GROUP OF *CHILDREN.*

"WHAT HAVE YOU BEEN DOING, MERRYLEGS?"

"OH, I HAD TO GIVE SOME YOUNG BOYS A *LESSON.* THE MASTER'S GIRLS ARE PROPER RIDERS, BUT THESE *BOYS,* THEY USED BIG STICKS AS *WHIPS.* SO I HAD TO BREAK THEM IN.

"WHEN THEY *WOULDN'T STOP* WHIPPING ME, WHY, I ROSE UP AND DUMPED THEM OFF, TO SHOW THEM THE *ERROR* OF THEIR WAYS."

25

"WHEN THEY BROUGHT ME TO JAMES, I THINK HE WAS ANGRY TO SEE THEIR *BIG STICKS.*"

"I WOULD HAVE GIVEN THOSE BOYS A *GOOD KICK,* THAT WOULD HAVE GIVEN THEM A *LESSON!*"

"HE TOLD THEM SUCH WHIPS WERE NOT FIT FOR YOUNG *GENTLEMEN.*"

"NO DOUBT YOU WOULD, GINGER, BUT I AM NOT QUITE SO *FOOLISH* AS THAT!

"DO YOU THINK I AM SUCH AN *UNGRATEFUL BRUTE* AS TO FORGET ALL THE KIND TREATMENT I HAVE HAD HERE? *NO!* AND IF YOU WERE SMART, YOU WOULD THINK THE SAME.

"BESIDES, IF I TOOK TO KICKING, WHERE WOULD I BE? *SOLD* OFF IN A JIFFY, TO WHO KNOWS WHAT SORT OF *ROUGH MASTER.* NO, THANK YOU, I SAY!"

CHAPTER 10: A TALK IN THE ORCHARD

ONE OF OUR GREATEST **PLEASURES** WAS TO CARRY THE MASTER AND HIS **FAMILY.** THE MASTER RODE GINGER, HIS LADY RODE ME, AND THEIR DAUGHTERS WERE ON SIR OLIVER AND MERRYLEGS.

THIS MADE GINGER CROSS WITH ME, AS SHE HAD TO CARRY THE **GREATER WEIGHT.** WHEN SHE COMPLAINED OF IT, OLD SIR OLIVER SAID:

"THERE, THERE, DON'T VEX YOURSELF! IT IS AN **HONOR** TO CARRY THE MASTER. WE HORSES MUST BE **CONTENT** AND WILLING SO LONG AS WE ARE KINDLY USED."

I HAD ALWAYS WONDERED HOW IT WAS THAT SIR OLIVER HAD SUCH A VERY **SHORT TAIL.** ON ONE OF OUR SUNDAY HOLIDAYS I VENTURED TO ASK HIM BY WHAT **ACCIDENT** IT WAS THAT HE HAD LOST IT.

"ACCIDENT!" HE SNORTED. "IT WAS **NO ACCIDENT!** IT WAS A CRUEL, SHAMEFUL, COLD BLOODED ACT OF MAN!"

"WHEN I WAS YOUNG, I WAS TIED UP, AND THEY **CUT OFF** MY LONG BEAUTIFUL TAIL, BONE AND ALL, AND THREW IT AWAY! AND ALL FOR THE SAKE OF **FASHION!** MEN LIKE THE LOOK OF BUTCHERY!"

"THEY DO THE SAME TO THEIR PETS. I HAD A DEAR FRIEND ONCE, A **TERRIER** WHO HAD HER PUPS IN MY STALL.

"ONE DAY THE PUPS WERE GONE, AND RETURNED WITH PIECES OF THEIR POOR LITTLE TAILS AND EARS **CUT OFF!** ALL DONE BY MAN FOR FASHION!"

"WHY DON'T THEY CUT THEIR OWN **CHILDREN'S EARS** INTO POINTS TO MAKE THEM LOOK SHARP? WHAT RIGHT HAVE THEY TO TORMENT AND **DISFIGURE** GOD'S CREATURES?" ASKED SIR OLIVER INDIGNANTLY.

TO CHANGE THE SUBJECT, I ASKED, "CAN ANYONE TELL ME THE USE OF **BLINKERS?**"

"NO," SAID SIR OLIVER, "BECAUSE THEY HAVE **NO USE!**"

"THEY ARE SUPPOSED TO KEEP HORSES FROM SEEING THINGS THAT WILL STARTLE THEM AND CAUSE **ACCIDENTS,**" SAID JUSTICE CALMLY.

"BLINKERS ARE **DANGEROUS THINGS** IN THE DARK," SAID SIR OLIVER STERNLY. "I RECALL ONE NIGHT WHEN THE MASTER'S CARRIAGE OVERTURNED..."

THINGS WERE GETTING **SORE** AGAIN WHEN MERRYLEGS HELD UP HIS WISE LITTLE HEAD AND SAID, "I BELIEVE THE WIND HAS BLOWN DOWN SOME **APPLES** AT THE ORCHARD, AND WE MIGHT AS WELL **EAT** THEM AS THE SLUGS."

MERRYLEG'S IDEA COULD NOT BE RESISTED, SO OFF WE WENT IN **SEARCH** OF SWEET APPLES TO LIFT OUR **SPIRITS.**

CHAPTER 12: A STORMY DAY

ONE DAY IN THE FALL, I CARRIED JOHN AND THE MASTER INTO TOWN. THERE HAD BEEN A *STORM* WITH MUCH RAIN, AND THE *WIND* WAS STILL GUSTING.

AT THE *TOLL*, THE RIVER WAS HIGH, NEARLY TOUCHING THE BOTTOM OF THE *BRIDGE*.

ON THE *RETURN TRIP*, THE WIND HAD PICKED UP, AND MADE A ROARING SOUND IN THE TREES.

I SAY, IT WOULD BE RATHER AWKWARD IF ONE OF THOSE *BRANCHES* CAME DOWN ON US!

RIGHT AT THAT MOMENT A *GREAT OAK* CAME CRASHING DOWN A SCANT FEW FEET IN FRONT OF US. I WAS *FRIGHTENED*, BUT DID NOT BUCK OR BOLT.

AFTER REGAINING OUR COMPOSURE, WE WENT LOOKING FOR ANOTHER ROUTE HOME.

IT WAS NEARLY *DARK* WHEN WE REACHED THE TOLL. THE WATER WAS VERY *HIGH*, COVERING THE CENTER OF THE BRIDGE.

THE MOMENT MY *HOOFS* TOUCHED THE BRIDGE, I KNEW SOMETHING WAS *WRONG*, AND I STOPPED.

GO ON, *BEAUTY!*

IT WAS SO *DARK* THEY COULD NOT *SEE* THE BRIDGE.

HE WORKED THE REINS IMPATIENTLY, BUT STILL I *DID NOT MOVE.*

WHAT IS IT, BEAUTY? WHAT'S THE *MATTER?*

HOY, STOP! THE BRIDGE IS BROKEN IN THE MIDDLE AND CARRIED AWAY! IF YOU COME ON YOU'LL BE SWEPT IN AS WELL!

FOR A LONG TIME DURING THE **DETOUR** HOME, MY MASTER SAID NOTHING. THEN...

GOD HAS GIVEN MAN **REASON**, BUT HE HAS GIVEN ANIMALS ANOTHER SENSE WE DO NOT POSSESS. I DO NOT KNOW WHAT TO NAME IT, BUT THAT **GIFT** HAS SAVED ALL OUR LIVES THIS NIGHT.

HERE YOU ARE **AT LAST!** THANK GOD!

IF NOT FOR BLACK BEAUTY, WE WOULD ALL BE AT THE BOTTOM OF THE **RIVER!**

NEVER WAS I SO GLAD TO LIE **SAFE** IN MY THICK BED OF STRAW, FOR I WAS OH SO TIRED!

CHAPTER 13: THE DEVIL'S TRADEMARK

ONE MORNING JOHN AND I CAME UPON A *BOY* WHIPPING A PONY, TRYING TO MAKE IT JUMP OVER A *HIGH GATE.*

THE PONY THREW THE BOY INTO A *THORN HEDGE* AND RAN AWAY.

HA HA! SERVES YOU RIGHT, BOY!

HAVE YOU SEEN MY SON, *JOHN?*

AYE, MR. BUSHBY, HE'S IN A HEDGE DOWN THE *ROAD*, WHERE HE BELONGS FOR BEATING HIS PONY.

I HOPE HE HAS LEARNED A *LESSON.*

AT HOME, JOHN TOLD *JAMES* ABOUT THE BOY.

SERVES HIM RIGHT INDEED. I KNEW HIM AT *SCHOOL.*

HE WAS THE SORT WHO LIKED PULLING THE *WINGS* OFF FLIES, TO WATCH THEM SUFFER.

THE *TEACHER* CAUGHT HIM, AND PUT HIM UP ON A *STOOL* FOR THE REST OF THE DAY, WEARING A *FOOL'S CAP.*

THEN HE TOLD US THAT SUCH PETTY CRUELTY WAS THE *DEVIL'S TRADEMARK*, AND SHOWED THAT A PERSON HAD NO LOVE OR RESPECT FOR MAN OR GOD.

A TRUE LESSON, JAMES. RELIGION IS A *SHAM* IF IT DOES NOT TEACH LOVE FOR ALL GOD'S CREATIONS, EH, BEAUTY?

GOOD MORNING, JOHN. I WANT TO KNOW IF YOU HAVE ANY *COMPLAINT* TO MAKE OF YOUNG JAMES

NO SIR, *NONE* AT ALL.

IF SOMEONE HAS BEEN TRYING TO *TAKE AWAY* HIS CHARACTER, I SAY THIS, SIR . . . I CAN *TRUST* HIS WORD AND I CAN TRUST HIS *WORK.*

WHOEVER WANTS TO KNOW THE CHARACTER OF JAMES HOWARD, LET THEM COME TO *JOHN MANLY.*

JAMES, MY BOY, MY BROTHER-IN-LAW IS IN NEED OF A *TRUSTWORTHY DRIVER.* I SHOULD HATE TO LOSE YOU, BUT IT WOULD BE A GOOD *STEP UP* FOR YOU, LAD.

THANK YOU, SIR. I SHALL *TAKE* IT!

AFTER THAT, WE WENT OUT NEARLY EVERY DAY SO THAT JAMES COULD *PRACTICE* HIS DRIVING.

JOHN MADE SURE THAT HE WAS AS WELL TRAINED AS POSSIBLE FOR HIS *NEW POSITION* IN LIFE.

37

CHAPTER 15: THE OLD OSTLER

MY MASTER AND MISTRESS DECIDED TO TAKE AN *OVERNIGHT TRIP* TO A DISTANT TOWN, AND JAMES WAS TO DRIVE THEM. WE ARRIVED AROUND SUNSET.

IN THE *HOTEL STABLE*, WE WERE ATTENDED BY AN OLD *OSTLER* , OR PROFESSIONAL GROOM. JAMES MARVELED AT HIS SURE HAND.

I SAY, YOU DO BEAT ALL FOR BEING QUICK AND *THOROUGH!*

PRACTICE MAKES PERFECT, AND *FORTY YEARS* OF IT I'VE HAD, HA HA! AND THESE WELL MANNERED HORSES OF YOURS MAKE IT EASY, LADDY.

WHO IS YOUR *MASTER*, IF I MIGHT ASK?

SQUIRE GORDON, OF BIRTWICK PARK.

AH, *POOR GENTLEMAN!* I READ IN THE PAPER OF HIS SON BEING KILLED, AND A FINE HORSE, TOO.

A MAN'S *LIFE* IS WORTH MORE THAN A FOX TAIL, AND HIS HORSE'S TOO, I MUST SAY!

CHAPTER 16: THE FIRE

THAT EVENING, A MAN WITH A *PIPE* WAS TALKING TO ONE OF THE OSTLERS. I PAID HIM NO HEED AND WENT TO *SLEEP*.

LATER I WOKE *CHOKING*, THE AIR ALL HOT AND THICK.

I HEARD A STRANGE *CRACKLING* NOISE THAT TERRIFIED ME.

THE *OTHERS* WERE ALL AWAKE, WHINNYING AND STAMPING THEIR FEET IN FEAR.

AN OSTLER APPEARED AND TRIED TO *PULL* ONE OF THE HORSES OUT, BUT HE WAS CRAZED WITH FEAR AND WOULD NOT MOVE.

THE NEXT THING I HEARD WAS *JAMES' VOICE*, QUIET AND CHEERFUL.

COME, IT IS TIME FOR US TO BE *OFF!*

HE TIED HIS *SCARF* OVER MY EYES TO CALM ME, AND LED ME OUT.

HERE, SOMEBODY! TAKE THIS HORSE WHILE I GO *BACK* FOR THE OTHER!

A TALL MAN TOOK ME, AND JAMES DARTED BACK INTO THE *STABLE.*

JAMES! JAMES HOWARD! ARE YOU THERE?

I WHINNIED AT THE SOUND OF MY *MASTER'S VOICE*, BUT THERE WAS NO OTHER ANSWER.

THE NEXT MOMENT I SAW JAMES COMING THROUGH THE SMOKE, LEADING *GINGER*. BOTH WERE *COUGHING* VIOLENTLY.

MY BRAVE LAD! ARE YOU *HURT?*

I AM *WELL*, SQUIRE.

AYE, HE IS A *BRAVE LAD*, AND NO MISTAKE!

"LET US GET OUT OF THE WAY THEN, FOR I HEAR THE *FIRE ENGINE* COMING!"

THERE WAS A DREADFUL *CRASH* AS THE ROOF COLLAPSED ON THE BURNING STABLE, AND THEN WE WERE AWAY IN THE FRESH NIGHT AIR.

JAMES, I MUST HASTEN TO YOUR MISTRESS. I TRUST IN YOU TO FIND NEW STABLES FOR THE HORSES. *GOOD NIGHT!*

THE NEXT DAY JAMES TOLD OF THE *MAN* WHO WAS SEEN ENTERING THE STABLE WITH A *PIPE*, AND EXITING WITHOUT IT. IT WAS THOUGHT THAT THIS WAS HOW THE FIRE HAD *STARTED.*

CHAPTER 17: JOHN MANLY'S TALK

THE REST OF OUR JOURNEY WAS *EASY*. MY MASTER'S FRIEND HAD A NICE, SNUG STABLE RUN BY A KIND GROOMSMAN. HE WAS MUCH *IMPRESSED* BY THE TALE OF THE FIRE.

IT'S CLEAR THOSE HORSES *TRUST* YOU LAD, ELSE THEY NEVER WOULD HAVE FOLLOWED YOU OUT OF THAT *FIRE*.

WE WERE SOON BACK *HOME*, AND GLAD TO BE THERE. JOHN AND JAMES HAD A *SERIOUS TALK* IN THE STABLE.

I SHALL BE *GONE* SOON, JOHN, I WONDER WHO WILL TAKE MY *PLACE?*

WHY, LITTLE JOE GREEN.

JOE GREEN! HE IS A *CHILD!*

HE IS *FOURTEEN*, THE SAME AGE I WAS WHEN MY PARENTS DIED. MY SISTER AND I WOULD NOT HAVE *MADE IT* HAD THE SQUIRE AND THE MISTRESS NOT LOOKED AFTER US.

JAMES, KINDNESS BREE[DS] *KINDNESS*, AND I AM SUR[E] GREEN WILL DO FINE HERE [AS] WILL YOU IN YOUR *NEW PL[ACE]*

JOE GREEN CAME TO THE STABLE THE *NEXT DAY*, TO LEARN ALL HE COULD FROM JAMES BEFORE HE LEFT.

AS HE WAS QUITE *TOO SHORT* TO GROOM HORSES, JAMES PUT HIM TO WORK LEARNING ON MERRYLEGS, WHO WAS A BIT PUT OUT AT BEING THE *PRACTICE PONY.*

TOO SOON, THE TIME CAME FOR JAMES TO *LEAVE* US.

THIS IS VERY HARD, JOHN. IF THE *EXTRA MONEY* WOULDN'T HELP MY MUM SO, I DON'T THINK I COULD DO IT.

TRUST IN *GOD* AND BE OF *GOOD CHEER*, LAD, AND ALL WILL BE WELL!

WE *MISSED* JAMES, MERRYLEGS MOST OF ALL. HE MOPED, AND WENT OFF HIS FEED.

TO CHEER HIM UP, JOHN AND I TOOK HIM OUT SEVERAL MORNINGS FOR A GOOD GALLOP, AND SOON HIS *SPIRITS* WERE HIGH AGAIN.

CHAPTER 18: GOING FOR THE DOCTOR

THERE IS NOT A MOMENT TO *WASTE*, JOHN, YOU RIDE FOR YOUR MISTRESS *LIFE!*

ONE NIGHT NOT LONG AFTER JAMES HAD LEFT, JOHN AND I HAD TO GO FOR THE DOCTOR, AS THE MISTRESS HAD TAKEN *ILL.*

THERE WAS BEFORE US A LONG PIECE OF *LEVEL ROAD* BY THE RIVERSIDE, AND FOR TWO MILES I GALLOPED AS FAST AS I COULD.

THE AIR WAS FROSTY, THE MOON WAS BRIGHT, AND AFTER ANOTHER EIGHT MILES, WE CAME TO THE *DOCTOR'S HOUSE.*

DOCTOR! WAKE UP! MRS. GORDON IS VERY *ILL*, YOU MUST COME AT ONCE!

OH MY!

MY SON IS AWAY ON MY HORSE! CAN I TAKE *YOURS?*

THE DOCTOR WAS A MUCH *HEAVIER MAN* THAN JOHN, AND NOT SO GOOD A RIDER.

BUT I DID MY BEST.

44

WHEN WE REACHED THE HOUSE, THE DOCTOR WENT RIGHT IN. JOE LED ME TO MY STALL, AND GAVE ME A PAIL FULL OF COLD WATER, THEN WENT AWAY.

SOON I BEGAN TO SHAKE AND TREMBLE, AND TURNED DEADLY COLD. HOW I WISHED FOR MY WARM, THICK BLANKET!

AFTER A LONG WHILE, I HEARD JOHN AT THE DOOR. I GAVE A LOW GROAN, AS I WAS IN GREAT PAIN.

HE QUICKLY COVERED ME WITH WARM BLANKETS, MUTTERING, "STUPID, STUPID BOY!"

THEN HE SAID, "MY POOR BEAUTY! YOU SAVE YOUR MISTRESS' LIFE, AND THIS IS YOUR REWARD!"

45

CHAPTER 20: JOE GREEN

I DID **RECOVER**, AND SO DID YOUNG JOE. HE TRIED TWICE AS HARD TO LEARN HIS JOB, AND SOON BEGAN TO BE **TRUSTED** WITH MANY TASKS.

WE WERE RETURNING FROM AN **ERRAND** WHEN WE CAME UPON A BRICK CART STUCK IN THE **MUD**.

THE **DRUNKEN DRIVER** WHIPPED THE HORSES MERCILESSLY, BUT THE CART WAS STUCK FAST.

PULL, YOU BRUTES!

WE STOPPED, AND YOUNG JOE **SPOKE UP**.

HEY NOW, IT DOES **NO GOOD** TO BE BEATING YOUR HORSES LIKE THAT!

MIND YOUR OWN BUSINESS, YOU IMPUDENT **WHELP!** GET ALONG WITH YOU!

47

WE TURNED AND WENT AT A GALLOP TO THE HOME OF THE **MASTER BRICKLAYER**.

MR. CLAY, THERE'S A FELLOW IN YOUR BRICKYARD FLOGGING TWO HORSES TO **DEATH!** I TOLD HIM TO STOP, BUT HE WOULDN'T! PRAY, SIR, **GO** NOW AND SEE TO IT!

THANK YE, LAD, I SHALL ATTEND TO IT **AT ONCE!**

WE FLEW HOME, AND IN ANGRY, EXCITED **WORDS** JOE TOLD JOHN WHAT HAD HAPPENED.

I'M ANGRY ALL OVER, I CAN TELL YOU!

YOU DID **RIGHT**, JOE. WITH SUCH CRUELTY IT IS **EVERYBODY'S BUSINESS** TO SPEAK UP!

48

JOE WAS GIVING ME A GOOD GROOMING WHEN **WORD** CAME DOWN THAT HE WAS TO REPORT DIRECTLY TO THE MASTER.

OUR MASTER WAS A **COUNTY MAGISTRATE,** AND THE CASE OF THE BRICK CART DRIVER WAS BEING BROUGHT BEFORE HIM. JOE STRAIGHTENED HIS NECKTIE AND WAS OFF TO GIVE HIS STATEMENT.

SPEAK WELL, LAD.

I **SHALL,** SIR!

WE HEARD LATER THAT JOE DID INDEED SPEAK WELL, AND THAT THE DRIVER WAS GIVEN THREE MONTHS IN **PRISON.**

A **CHANGE** CAME OVER JOE AFTER THAT. HE WAS JUST AS KIND AS BEFORE, BUT THERE WAS MORE **PURPOSE** TO ALL THAT HE DID. IT SEEMED AS IF HE HAD JUMPED AT ONCE FROM A BOY INTO A **MAN.**

CHAPTER 21: THE PARTING

I HAD NOW LIVED IN THIS HAPPY PLACE FOR THREE YEARS, BUT **SAD CHANGES** WERE COMING. THE MISTRESS WAS GRAVELY **ILL**, AND THE DOCTOR ADVISED HER TO MOVE TO A WARMER CLIMATE.

THE MASTER BEGAN TO MAKE PLANS FOR THE **SALE** OF HIS PROPERTY, INCLUDING US.

THE MASTER'S TWO DAUGHTERS **LEFT** FIRST, ALONG WITH THEIR GOVERNESS. THEY CRIED WHEN THEY HUGGED POOR MERRYLEGS **GOODBYE**.

HE WAS TO BE GIVEN TO THE VICAR, ON THE CONDITION THAT JOE BE ENGAGED TO CARE FOR HIM.

GINGER AND I WERE TO BE SOLD TO THE MASTER'S FRIEND, THE **EARL OF WHITE**. THE EVENING BEFORE THEY LEFT, THE MASTER CAME TO THE STABLE. BOTH HE AND JOHN WERE IN **LOW SPIRITS**.

HAVE YOU DECIDED WHAT TO **DO**, JOHN?

I HAVE MADE UP MY MIND TO **TRAIN** YOUNG HORSES FULL TIME. MANY YOUNG ANIMALS ARE RUINED BY **WRONG TREATMENT.**

I THINK I COULD HELP THEM GET OFF TO A **BETTER START.** WHAT DO YOU THINK, SIR?

I DON'T KNOW A MAN ANYWHERE WHO COULD MAKE A *BETTER JOB* OF IT, JOHN. IF I CAN *HELP* IN ANY WAY, PLEASE WRITE.

THANK YOU, SIR. I PRAY *GOD* THAT WE MAY *SEE* YOU BACK ON THESE SHORES AGAIN ONE DAY.

THE LAST SAD DAY HAD COME. THERE WERE MANY *TEARS SHED* AS GINGER AND I PULLED OUR MASTER AND MISTRESS FOR THE FINAL TIME.

WE TROTTED SLOWLY THROUGH THE *VILLAGE* WHERE THE PEOPLE WERE STANDING AT THEIR DOORS TO HAVE ONE *LAST LOOK* AND TO SAY, "GOD BLESS THEM."

ALL OUR *HEARTS* WERE TOO HEAVY FOR LONG GOODBYES. THE MASTER AND MISTRESS QUICKLY BOARDED THEIR *CAR*, THE DOORS SLAMMED SHUT, AND THE TRAIN GLIDED AWAY.

WE SHALL NEVER SEE THEM AGAIN, JOE. *NEVER!*

NEITHER JOHN NOR JOE COULD HOLD BACK THEIR *TEARS* AS THE TRAIN STEAMED FROM SIGHT.

THE NEXT MORNING, JOHN TOOK GINGER US TO **EARLSHALL PARK,** WHERE THE EARL OF WHITE LIVED. THERE WAS A FINE LARGE HOUSE, AND A GREAT DEAL OF STABLING.

JOHN MET WITH **MR. YORK,** THE HEAD COACHMAN, AND THEY HAD A **TALK** ABOUT US.

THE BLACK ONE HAS THE MOST **PERFECT TEMPERAMENT** I HAVE EVER KNOWN.

THE OTHER MUST HAVE HAD SOME **ROUGH TREATMENT** BEFORE SHE CAME TO US, AND SHE CAN BE HIGH STRUNG. IF SHE IS ILL TREATED, SHE WILL GIVE TIT FOR TAT.

I SHOULD ALSO MENTION THAT WE NEVER USED THE **BEARING REIN** ON EITHER OF THEM, AND I DOUBT THAT GINGER WOULD TAKE IT WELL.

WELL, I WILL SPEAK TO MY LORD ABOUT IT, BUT THE LADY OF THE HOUSE **INSISTS** ON THE REINS.

I AM VERY SORRY TO HEAR IT, BUT I MUST BE **OFF,** OR I WILL MISS THE **TRAIN.**

THE NEXT AFTERNOON WE WERE **HARNESSED** TO THE CARRIAGE WITH THE BEARING REINS LOOSELY FITTED AND BOUGHT TO THE FRONT OF THE HOUSE. THE **LADY** APPEARED, AND STEPPED UP TO **INSPECT** US.

SHE WAS A TALL, **PROUD-LOOKING WOMAN,** AND SHE DID NOT LOOK PLEASED, BUT SHE SAID NOTHING.

THUS WAS I INTRODUCED TO THE DREADEDBEARING REINS. THEY WERE QUITE **UNPLEASANT,** BUT I THOUGHT I COULD STAND THEM, AND SAID SO TO GINGER.

"NOW YOU SEE WHAT IT IS LIKE! BUT THEY ARE NOT **TOO TIGHT,** AND IF IT GETS NO WORSE, I SHALL TAKE IT," SAID GINGER.

THE **NEXT DAY** WE WERE AGAIN BROUGHT ROUND FOR THE LADY. THIS TIME SHE SPOKE IN AN IMPERIOUS VOICE.

YORK, YOU **MUST** PUT THESE HORSES' HEADS UP **HIGHER**, THEY ARE NOT FIT TO BE SEEN!

I SHALL TAKE THEM UP BUT A LITTLE, YOUR LADYSHIP, FOR MY LORD SAID TO BRING THEM UP **SLOWLY**, AS THESE HORSES ARE NOT USED TO THE REINS.

GINGER WAS **NOT HAPPY** WITH THIS, AND SAID, "IF THEY STRAIN ME UP TIGHT, WHY, LET 'EM LOOK OUT! I CAN'T BEAR IT, AND I WON'T!"

BECAUSE OF THE BEARING REINS, PULLING THE *CARRIAGE* WAS NO LONGER A PLEASURE. BUT *WORSE* WAS TO COME. ONE DAY . . .

YORK, *RAISE* THOSE HORSES' HEADS ALL THE WAY *UP!*

YES, MY LADY.

THE MOMENT YORK BEGAN TO *TIGHTEN* THE REINS ON GINGER, SHE *EXPLODED.*

SHE REARED AND *KICKED* SO WILDLY THAT SHE BROKE *LOOSE* FROM THE CARRIAGE AND FELL TO THE GROUND.

I WAS UNHOOKED FROM THE CARRIAGE AND PUT INTO MY *STALL* STILL IN FULL HARNESS. GINGER LAY ON THE GROUND *ENTANGLED* IN HER HARNESS.

CUT HER *LOOSE* AND GET HER INTO HER STALL!

LATER, YORK MUTTERED SULLENLY TO HIMSELF AS HE WAS *INSPECTING* ME.

I KNEW *MISCHIEF* WOULD COME OF THOSE REINS! HMM, NOTHING BROKEN, JUST SOME BRUISES, GOOD, GOOD.

55

LORD WHITE WAS MUCH **PUT OUT** WHEN HE LEARNED WHAT HAD HAPPENED. HE AND YORK DECIDED THAT GINGER WOULD NEVER AGAIN BE PUT INTO THE CARRIAGE. **OTHER WORK** WOULD BE FOUND FOR HER.

WHEN I WAS RECOVERED, I WAS PUT BACK INTO SERVICE WITH A NEW PARTNER NAMED **MAX.** THE BEARING REINS WERE FITTED AS TIGHTLY AS EVER. I ASKED MAX HOW HE COULD **STAND IT.**

"WELL, I BEAR IT BECAUSE I **MUST**, THAT IS HOW. IT IS SHORTENING MY LIFE, AND IT WILL SHORTEN YOURS TOO, IF YOU HAVE TO **STICK** TO IT. SUCH IS OUR LOT, WHAT ELSE CAN WE DO BUT BEAR IT?" HE SAID.

I SAID NOTHING, BUT THOUGHT OF GINGER'S **REPLY** TO THE REINS. BUT EVEN SHE HAD NOT ESCAPED CRUEL FATE.

56

THE DOCTOR'S HOUSE WAS ONLY A MILE AWAY, AND WE HAD A **PLEASANT TROT** TO HIS GATE.

I SHALL **WAIT** FOR YOU HERE.

AS YOU WISH, I WON'T BE A **MINUTE.**

ALL WAS **QUIET** FOR A MOMENT, BUT THEN A BOY APPEARED, DRIVING SEVERAL YOUNG **COLTS** WITH A WHIP. THEY WERE WILD AND **UNRULY**, DASHING TO AND FRO.

ONE OF THEM **BOLTED**, BLUNDERING INTO LIZZIE, AND STARTLING HER.

LIZZIE **PANICKED**, AND DASHED OFF IN A HEADLONG **GALLOP**.

LADY ANNE COULD NOT STOP HER.

I GAVE A LOUD **SHRILL NEIGH**, AND BLANTYRE APPEARED AT THE GATE, JUST IN TIME TO CATCH SIGHT OF THE **RUNAWAY** PAIR.

HE SPRANG INTO THE SADDLE AND WE WERE OFF IN **WILD PURSUIT** OF THE FARAWAY FIGURES.

WE LOST SIGHT OF THEM AT AN INTERSECTION, BUT A *LOCAL WOMAN* POINTED THE WAY.

TO THE *RIGHT*, M'LORD!

FOR A MOMENT WE CAUGHT SIGHT OF THEM, BUT ANOTHER *BEND* AND THEY WERE *HIDDEN* AGAIN.

I WAS GOING *FLAT OUT*, BUT WE SCARCELY SEEMED TO BE *GAINING* ANY GROUND ON THEM.

THIS TIME AN OLD MAN POINTED THE WAY. LIZZIE HAD GONE OFF THE *ROAD* INTO THE COUNTRYSIDE.

WE SAW THEM AND BEGAN TO GET *CLOSER*, AS THE ROUGH FOOTING CAUSED LIZZIE TO *SLOW* SOME.

THEN WE SAW A NEWLY DUG *DIKE* BEFORE US. SURELY LIZZIE WOULD STOP NOW!

BUT LIZZIE DID NOT SLOW DOWN. SHE CLEARED THE DIKE WITH A *WILD LEAP.*

THERE WAS MUCH *LOOSE EARTH* ON THE FAR SIDE, AND LIZZIE *STUMBLED*, THROWING THE LADY ANNE ROUGHLY TO THE GROUND.

ANNE!

BLANTYRE GENTLY ROLLED HER OVER. THERE WAS *NO BLOOD*, BUT SHE DID NOT MOVE.

TWO MEN WHO HAD BEEN *WORKING* NEARBY RAN TO US.

HELP, *HERE!* QUICKLY, PLEASE!

CAN YOU *RIDE*, MAN?

I AIN'T MUCH OF A HORSEMAN, SIR, BUT I WILL DO *MY BEST* FOR THE LADY ANNE!

THE MAN HAD SPOKEN **TRUE**, BUT HE DID MANAGE TO **HANG ON** AS WE MADE OUR WAY BACK TO THE DOCTOR'S, AND THEN ON TO EARLSHALL.

IT WAS A WILD RIDE, AND I WAS **DONE IN** BY THE TIME WE GOT HOME.

I WAS UNSADDLED AND PUT AWAY IN **GREAT HASTE**. A MAN WAS SENT ON GINGER TO HEAR THE DOCTOR'S **REPORT** ON LADY ANNE.

WHEN SHE WAS **RETURNED** TO HER STALL, GINGER TOLD ME WHAT SHE HAD HEARD.

"I CAN'T TELL YOU MUCH," SHE SAID. "THE DOCTOR FIRST PRONOUNCED THAT SHE WAS NOT DEAD. HE SAID SHE HAD NO BROKEN BONES. THEY TOOK HER AWAY IN THE CARRIAGE. WE CAN ONLY HOPE FOR THE BEST."

LATER, BLANTYRE VISITED AND TOLD ME THAT LADY ANNE WOULD **RECOVER**, AS THOUGH HE KNEW I WOULD **UNDERSTAND**. I DID INDEED, AND LOOKED FORWARD TO MANY MORE HAPPY RIDES WITH HER

64

CHAPTER 25: REUBEN SMITH

REUBEN SMITH WAS YORK'S **SECOND-IN-COMMAND.** HE RAN THE STABLE WHENEVER YORK WAS AWAY. HE WAS STEADY, ABLE, AND QUITE **KNOWLEDGEABLE** IN THE HORSE BUSINESS.

HE SHOULD HAVE BEEN A **HEAD COACHMAN** HIMSELF, BUT HE HAD ONE PROBLEM: HE WAS SOMETIMES TOO FOND OF **DRINK.**

REUBEN RODE ME INTO TOWN ON BUSINESS ON SATURDAY. HIS **ERRANDS** COMPLETED. HE HANDED ME OVER TO AN OSTLER AND WENT INTO A **PUB,** NOT TO RETURN FOR **MANY HOURS.**

WHEN HE DID RETURN, IT WAS DARK, AND HE WAS **QUITE DRUNK.**

THE OSTLER TOLD REUBEN I HAD A **LOOSE SHOE.** HIS ONLY REPLY WAS A **CURSE.**

HE MOUNTED **AWKWARDLY** AND WHIPPED ME INTO A **GALLOP.** SHOUTED WARNINGS WENT **UNHEEDED.**

THOUGH IT WAS QUITE DARK AND THE ROAD *ROUGH*, REUBEN KEPT ME WHIPPED UP TO A *FULL GALLOP*.

THE *ROAD* HAD RECENTLY BEEN *REDONE* WITH LARGE, SHARP STONES, AND GOING OVER IT AT THIS SPEED *LOOSENED* MY SHOE FURTHER.

THE *LOOSE SHOE* FINALLY CAUGHT ON A *STONE* AND CAME OFF ENTIRELY.

HAD REUBEN NOT BEEN *MAD DRUNK*, HE WOULD HAVE NOTICED AND *SLOWED* OUR PACE.

AS IT WAS, A *FALL* WAS *INEVITABLE*.

WE HIT THE *HARD STONES* WITH GREAT FORCE.

REUBEN *GROANED* ONCE AND WAS *STILL*. I WAS IN TREMENDOUS *PAIN* MYSELF, BUT THERE WAS *NOTHING* I COULD DO BUT BEAR IT UNTIL SOMEONE CAME ALONG.

CHAPTER 26: HOW IT ENDED

AT LAST, I HEARD THE DISTANT **SOUND** OF A HORSES' FEET ON STONE. IT WAS **GINGER**, PULLING A CART BEARING TWO MEN FROM **EARLSHALL**.

THEY RUSHED TO REUBEN AND FOUND HIM AS **COLD** AS THE STONE UPON WHICH HE LAY. HE WAS QUITE **DEAD**.

THEY SOLEMNLY LOADED HIM INTO THE **CART**, THEN CAME TO **EXAMINE** ME.

NOTICING **MY MISSING SHOE** AND DAMAGED HOOF, AND KNOWING OF REUBEN'S **PROBLEM** WITH DRINK, THEY PUZZLED OUT THE EVENTS THAT HAD LED TO THIS **SAD SCENE**.

ONE OF THE MEN LED ME BACK THE **THREE MILES** TO EARLSHALL.

I SHALL NEVER FORGET THAT SLOW, **AGONIZING WALK** HOME AS LONG AS I SHALL LIVE.

IN ADDITION TO THE GASHES ON MY KNEES, MY *HOOF* HAD BEEN CUT TO *PIECES.* MY *RECOVERY* WAS SLOW AND *PAINFUL.* EVEN IF I COULD WORK AGAIN, I WOULD BE *SCARRED* FOR LIFE.

AN *INQUEST* WAS HELD. AFTER ALL THE *EVIDENCE* WAS PRESENTED TO THE *MAGISTRATE,* I WAS CLEARED OF ALL *BLAME.*

EVERYONE *PITIED* REUBEN'S WIFE SUSAN. SHE AND HER SIX YOUNG CHILDREN HAD TO *LEAVE* THEIR PLEASANT HOUSE BY THE TALL OAK TREES, AND GO INTO THE GREAT GLOOMY *UNION HOUSE.*

CHAPTER 27: RUINED AND GOING DOWNHILL

AS SOON AS MY KNEES **HEALED** SOME, I WAS PUT INTO A **SMALL MEADOW** FOR A MONTH.

IT WAS PLEASANT TO BE FREE OF WORK, BUT I HAD NO COMPANY, AND MISSED GINGER GREATLY.

IMAGINE MY **PLEASURE** THEN WHEN ONE MORNING GINGER WAS **TURNED OUT** WITH ME.

BUT IT WAS NOT FOR THE SAKE OF **COMPANY** THAT SHE HAD BEEN PUT IN WITH ME. SHE TOO HAD BEEN **RUINED** BY HARD USE.

AFTER THE **CARRIAGE INCIDENT**, SHE HAD BEEN USED AS A **HUNTING HORSE** BY THE EARL'S FOOLISH SON GEORGE, AND HE HAD **WORN HER OUT.**

"AND SO **HERE** WE ARE," SAID GINGER, "**RUINED** IN THE PRIME OF OUR YOUTH AND STRENGTH. YOU BY A **DRUNKARD**, AND I BY A **FOOL!** IT IS VERY HARD TO BEAR!"

THOUGH WE BOTH KNEW WE WERE NOT WHAT WE HAD BEEN, THAT DID NOT KEEP US FROM **ENJOYING** OUR COMPANY, AT LEAST FOR A **BRIEF** WHILE.

THEN ONE DAY THE EARL AND YORK CAME INTO THE MEADOW TO *INSPECT* US. THE EARL SEEMED MOST *ANNOYED.*

TWO GOOD HORSES RUINED, AND I *PROMISED* THE SQUIRE THEY WOULD HAVE A *GOOD HOME!* THE MARE MAY YET RECOVER, BUT THE BLACK MUST *GO.* I CAN'T HAVE KNEES LIKE THOSE IN MY STABLE!

IF I MAY, M'LORD, I KNOW A *LIVERY STABLE OWNER* WHO TREATS HIS HORSES WELL, AND CARES LITTLE ABOUT APPEARANCE, SO LONG AS THE HORSE IS SOUND. I WILL CONTACT HIM.

A WEEK LATER I WAS *SOLD,* AND A MAN CAME TO TAKE ME *AWAY* TO THE LIVERY STABLES.

I NEIGHED *GOODBYE* TO GINGER, AND SHE SAID: "AND NOW I LOSE THE ONLY FRIEND I HAVE! 'TIS A *HARD WORLD!*"

AT THE END OF MY *JOURNEY,* I FOUND MYSELF AT A *TOLERABLE STABLE.* SOON I WOULD LEARN WHAT MY NEW *JOB* WAS TO BE.

CHAPTER 28: A JOB-HORSE
AND HIS DRIVERS

A LIVERY STABLE HAS HORSES AND CARRIAGES FOR *RENT*. SOMETIMES DRIVERS ARE *HIRED*, OTHER TIMES THE *CUSTOMERS* DRIVE THEMSELVES.

I HAD ALWAYS BEEN DRIVEN BY *PROFESSIONALS*, BUT NOW I WAS TO EXPERIENCE THE WORST KIND OF BAD AND *IGNORANT DRIVERS*.

SOME WERE *NERVOUS*, OTHERS LAZY, AND STILL OTHERS *MEAN*. BUT I FELT THE *WORST* WERE THOSE WHO WERE JUST ALTOGETHER *CARELESS*.

I WAS OUT WITH ONE SUCH *DRIVER* AND HIS FAMILY WHEN I GOT A *STONE* STUCK IN MY HOOF.

ANYONE WITH A WHIT OF *SENSE* WOULD HAVE NOTICED MY *GAIT* WAS OFF, BUT NOT THIS FELLOW. LUCKILY FOR ME, WE MET A *KINDLY FARMER.*

HALLO THERE, YOUR HORSE HAS A BIT OF A *LIMP*, MIND IF I TAKE A LOOK?

HELP YOUR-SELF, MY GOOD FELLOW.

WITH A *PRACTICED HAND*, THE FARMER DUG THE STONE OUT.

BLESS ME, WHAT A *BOULDER!* SMALL WONDER YOU'RE *LIMPING!*

GOT IT! BUT YOU'D BEST TAKE IT EASY ON HIM, SIR.

BUT OF COURSE THE DRIVER POPPED HIS *WHIP* AS SOON AS THE FARMER WAS OUT OF SIGHT.

IMAGINE THAT! I NEVER KNEW THAT HORSES PICKED UP STONES LIKE THAT! ON WITH YOU NOW!

THIS WAS THE SORT OF DRIVER WE *JOB-HORSES* HAD TO PUT UP WITH.

Another bad sort of driving is the **STEAM ENGINE STYLE.** These drivers seem to think a horse should be able to go for miles **WITHOUT TIRING,** rain or shine, like a steam **LOCOMOTIVE.**

CHAPTER 29: COCKNEYS

But the **WORST** are the people from **COCKNEY.** Rory and I were returning **HOME** one evening when we had a **RUN-IN** with a Cockney.

Suddenly, a small cart burst from behind a **BLIND HEDGE,** coming right at us.

We could not get out of the way, and poor Rory was **SPEARED** with the gig shaft!

Rory eventually **HEALED,** but he was never the same, and was **SOLD OFF.**

AFTER RORY, I WAS PAIRED WITH A MARE NAMED *PEGGY.* SHE WAS A GOOD SORT, BUT SHE HAD AN *ODD PACE* THAT MADE HER HARD TO WORK WITH.

WHEN WE GOT HOME, I *ASKED* HER ABOUT IT.

"AH," SHE REPLIED, "IT IS THESE *SHORT LEGS* OF MINE, THEY MAKE ME GO SLOWLY, AND THEN IT IS *WHIP, WHIP, WHIP,* ALL THE TIME, SO THEN I GO TOO FAST. IF ONLY MY LEGS WERE LONGER!"

BUT PEGGY EVENTUALLY HAD SOME *LUCK:* SHE WAS SOLD TO TWO LADIES WHO LIKED HER *SLOW PACE,* AND SHE LOOKED QUITE HAPPY THEREAFTER.

PEGGY WAS REPLACED BY A YOUNG FELLOW WHO HAD A **BAD REPUTATION** FOR SHYING AND STARTING. I ASKED HIM WHY THIS WAS SO.

"WHEN I WAS YOUNG I WANTED TO **LOOK** AT THINGS, WHICH IS HARD TO DO WITH **BLINKERS** ON. BUT MY MASTER BEAT ME WHEN I LOOKED. NOW I AM AFRAID OF **ANYTHING** I CAN'T SEE.

"ONCE WHEN HE WAS **WHIPPING** ME FOR LOOKING THE OLD FELLOW WITH HIM **PROTESTED**, SO I SUPPOSE MEN ARE NOT ALL BAD.

"I DON'T MEAN TO **SHY**, BUT HOW SHOULD ONE KNOW WHAT IS **DANGEROUS** AND WHAT IS NOT, IF ONE IS NEVER ALLOWED TO LOOK AT ANYTHING?"

THE MORE I LEARNED OF MEN AND THEIR WAYS, THE MORE I **APPRECIATED** FARMER GRAY AND SQUIRE GORDON.

BUT AS THE YOUNG FELLOW SAID, THEY ARE NOT *ALL BAD.* ONE MORNING I WAS HIRED BY A MAN WHO ACTUALLY *LOOSENED* UP MY BIT AND REINS.

I ARCHED MY BACK AND SET OFF AT MY *BEST PACE.* IT WAS A PLEASURE TO BE DRIVEN BY SOMEONE WHO KNEW WHAT THEY WERE DOING.

THIS GENTLEMAN TOOK A GREAT *LIKING* TO ME. HE CONVINCED MY MASTER TO SELL ME TO A FRIEND OF HIS. AND SO IT CAME TO PASS THAT IN THE SUMMER I WAS SOLD TO *MR. BARRY.*

MR. BARRY WAS A KIND MASTER, BUT HE KNEW LITTLE ABOUT HORSES.

HE BOARDED ME IN A STABLE NEAR HIS HOME AND ORDERED THAT I BE GIVEN GOOD CARE AND THE *BEST FOOD.*

AT FIRST THE OLD GROOM FOLLOWED HIS ORDERS, BUT SOON HE BEGAN TO CUT BACK ON MY FOOD, AND TO *SUBSTITUTE* GRASS FOR OATS AND CORN. I BEGAN TO FEEL WEAK FROM THIS *POOR DIET.*

CHAPTER 31: A HUMBUG

MY MASTER SOON HIRED A **NEW GROOM**, BUT HE WAS NO BETTER THAN THE LAST ONE.

HE CONSIDERED HIMSELF QUITE HANDSOME, AND SPENT MORE TIME **PRIMPING** IN THE MIRROR THAN HE DID LOOKING AFTER ME.

WHEN MY MASTER WAS AROUND, THE GROOM WAS QUITE ATTENTIVE, BUT WENT BACK TO HIS **PREENING** WHEN MR. BARRY HAD GONE.

THE WORST OF IT WAS THAT HE NEVER **CLEANED** OUT MY STALL PROPERLY, SO THAT IT BECAME A DAMP, SMELLY **MESS**.

MY FEET SOON BECAME SORE AND **INFECTED** FROM STANDING IN THIS **MUCK**.

MR. BARRY NOTICED NONE OF THIS UNTIL I *STUMBLED* ONE DAY AND NEARLY THREW HIM.

HE TOOK ME TO THE NEAREST *BLACKSMITH* TO SEE WHAT THE MATTER WAS.

ALL HIS HOOVES ARE BADLY INFECTED. USUALLY COMES FROM A *FILTHY STALL*. I'D SAY YOUR GROOM HAS NOT BEEN DOING HIS JOB, SIR.

MR. BARRY WAS SO *DISGUSTED* AT HAVING BEEN TAKEN IN BY TWO BAD GROOMS THAT HE DECIDED TO SELL ME.

AS SOON AS MY FEET HEALED, I WAS TURNED OVER TO A *DEALER* TO BE SOLD AT A HORSE FAIR.

BUT HIS *OFFER* FOR ME WAS *REFUSED,* AND ONE OF THE ROUGHER SORTS BEGAN TO *HAGGLE* FOR ME.

BUT BEFORE THE *DEAL* COULD BE CLOSED, THE QUIET MAN RETURNED AND OFFERED *MORE.*

AND YOU MAY *DEPEND* UPON IT THERE'S A MONSTROUS DEAL OF *QUALITY* IN THAT HORSE.

THUS WAS I *PURCHASED* BY ONE JERRY BARKER, A PROFESSIONAL *CABBY* FROM LONDON.

IT WAS A LONG JOURNEY BACK TO *LONDON*, AND MANY STRANGE SITES MET MY EYES WHEN WE CAME TO THE *OUTSKIRTS.*

WE CONTINUED ON FOR *MILES*, AND IT BEGAN TO GROW *DARK.*

AT LAST WE CAME TO A NARROW STREET WITH RATHER *SHABBY HOUSES*, AND MY MASTER LET OUT A LOUD *WHISTLE.*

A YOUNG WOMAN AND TWO *CHILDREN* BURST FROM A NEARBY DOOR AND RAN TO *GREET* US.

THIS WAS JERRY'S *FAMILY.* HIS WIFE POLLY, HIS SON HARRY, AND HIS LITTLE GIRL, DOLLY.

THEY WERE NOW MY FAMILY AS WELL, AND THEY MADE ME FEEL RIGHT AT *HOME.*

83

CHAPTER 33: A LONDON CAB HORSE

JERRY'S FAMILY WAS A *HAPPY* ONE, AND THEY TREATED ME WELL. THEY CALLED ME *JACK*, AFTER ANOTHER BLACK HORSE THEY HAD OWNED.

PULLING THE *CAB* WAS NOT TOO DIFFERENT FROM *CART DUTY*, AND THERE WAS NO BEARING REIN TO CONTEND WITH.

AT THE CAB STAND, I WAS *INSPECTED* BY JERRY'S FELLOW CABBIES. I GOT THE SEAL OF *APPROVAL* FROM *GOVERNOR GRANT*, THE OLDEST OF THE CABBIES.

HE'S A *GOOD SORT*, JERRY. WHATEVER YOU GAVE FOR HIM, HE'LL BE *WORTH* IT.

MY FIRST WEEK AS A *LONDON CAB HORSE* WAS VERY TRYING, AS I WAS NOT USED TO THE *NOISE*, AND ALL THE CROWDS OF PEOPLE AND HORSES I HAD TO MAKE MY WAY THROUGH.

BUT JERRY WAS A *GOOD DRIVER*, AND I SOON CAME TO TRUST HIM, AND LEARNED TO DO MY JOB WELL.

JERRY HAD ANOTHER HORSE NAMED *CAPTAIN*, A NOBLE OLD HORSE WHO HAD SERVED IN THE *CRIMEAN WAR.*

ON ONE OF OUR SUNDAY'S OFF, HE TOLD ME HIS *STORY.*

85

"I WAS BROKEN IN AND TRAINED TO BE AN *ARMY HORSE*," CAPTAIN SAID. "MY FIRST AND DEAREST MASTER WAS A *CAVALRY OFFICER*.

"WHEN IT CAME TIME TO SHIP OUT, WE WERE *BLINDFOLDED* AND SWUNG ABOARD A GREAT VESSEL. AFTER A LONG, UNPLEASANT *JOURNEY*, WE CAME TO A LAND CALLED THE *CRIMEA*.

"IT WAS A COLD, *UNCOMFORTABLE PLACE*, BUT OUR MASTERS DID ALL THEY COULD TO KEEP US WELL, SO IT WAS NOT SO BAD."

"BUT WHAT ABOUT THE *FIGHTING?*" I ASKED. "WAS THAT NOT WORSE THAN ANYTHING ELSE?"

HE REPLIED, "WE BELIEVED SO LONG AS OUR *MASTERS* SAT FIRM IN THE SADDLE, WE HAD NOTHING TO *FEAR* FROM BOMB OR BULLET, AND SO IT WAS AT THE BEGINNING."

"MY NOBLE MASTER AND I CAME THROUGH MANY *ACTIONS* TOGETHER WITHOUT A *SCRATCH,* ALTHOUGH I DID SEE MANY A BRAVE MAN AND HORSE GO *DOWN.*

"WE RODE FIELDS WHERE THE *SHELLS* FELL THICK AS FLIES AND THE GROUND WAS SLICK WITH *BLOOD,* BUT I NEVER FELT *TERROR* UNTIL ONE DREADFUL DAY."

"WE AROSE AT **SUNRISE** ONE FINE AUTUMN DAY AND PREPARED FOR **ACTION.** AS THE LIGHT INCREASED, THERE SEEMED TO BE SOME **EXCITEMENT** AMONG THE OFFICERS.

"MY DEAR MASTER AND I WERE AT THE HEAD OF THE **LINE.** HE SEEMED DISTRACTED THAT MORNING, AND STROKED MY NECK MORE THAN USUAL.

"I CANNOT TELL ALL THAT **HAPPENED** ON THAT DAY, BUT I WILL TELL OF THE **LAST CHARGE** WE MADE.

"NEVER HAD WE BEEN UNDER SUCH A **FIRE** AS WE RODE THROUGH THAT DAY, BUT NOT A MAN NOR HORSE FALTERED!"

"FROM THE *RIGHT*, FROM THE *LEFT*, AND FROM THE *FRONT*, SHELLS POURED IN UPON US! MY MASTER WAS TORN FROM THE SADDLE BY A MIGHTY *BLAST*.

"I WANTED TO *STAY* BY HIS SIDE, BUT I WAS DRIVEN OFF BY THE THUNDERING *EXPLOSIONS*.

"I FLED IN BLIND *TERROR* FROM THE MADNESS OF THE BATTLEFIELD.

"I NEVER SAW MY DEAR MASTER AGAIN."

"STRANGE," I SAID. "I HAVE HEARD SOME MEN SPEAK OF WAR AS IF IT WERE A VERY *FINE THING*."

"AH," HE REPLIED. "THEY HAVE *NEVER SEEN* WHAT I HAVE, OR THEY WOULD SAY OTHERWISE."

CHAPTER 35: JERRY BARKER

I NEVER KNEW A *BETTER MAN* THAN JERRY BARKER. HE AND HIS FAMILY WERE ALWAYS *SINGING* AND LAUGHING EVEN WHEN THEY WERE HARD AT *WORK*.

THE ONLY THING THAT MADE JERRY CROSS WERE *PUSHY PEOPLE* IN A HURRY FOR NO GOOD REASON.

CABBIE! AN *EXTRA SHILLING* FOR A QUICK RIDE TO THE STATION!

SORRY, WE'RE ALL OUT OF *QUICK RIDES*, TRY MY MATE.

ALTHOUGH JERRY WAS SET AGAINST RUSHING FOR *NOTHING*, HE COULD PUT ON THE *STEAM* IF HE HAD A *GOOD REASON*.

ONE MORNING A MAN HAILED US BUT *SLIPPED* ON AN ORANGE AND TOOK A *HARD FALL.*

THE POOR FELLOW WAS QUITE *STUNNED,* BUT SEEMED DETERMINED TO MAKE THE *12 O'CLOCK TRAIN.*

JERRY TOOK *PITY* ON THE CHAP AND PROMISED TO GET HIM TO THE STATION *ON TIME.*

THERE WAS QUITE A BIT OF *TRAFFIC*, AND IT WAS A *NEAR THING*, BUT WE GOT HIM THERE WITH MOMENTS TO *SPARE*.

HE OFFERED JERRY A *HANDSOME TIP*, BUT JERRY TOOK ONLY HIS *USUAL FARE*, SAYING IT WAS HIS *GOOD DEED* FOR THE DAY.

BACK AT THE *CAB STAND*, WE TOOK SOME *RIBBING* WHEN JERRY TOLD THE TALE.

YOU'LL NEVER BE A *RICH MAN*, MATE!

FEH, WE KNOW WHAT THE *GOOD BOOK* SAYS ABOUT RICH MEN AND HEAVEN, EH, JERRY?

WHEN **WORD** SPREAD THAT JERRY HAD LOST HIS **BEST CUSTOMER**, THERE WAS MUCH **DEBATE** OVER IT AT THE CAB STAND.

I STILL SAY YOU'LL NEVER BE **RICH**, JERRY.

AND I SAY **GOOD** FOR YOU, IT IS OUR RIGHT TO HAVE A DAY OF **REST**.

NONE OF US WOULD BE OUT ON SUNDAYS IF **RICH FOLK** DIDN'T NEED RIDES TO **CHURCH**. I SHALL EXPECT THEM TO ANSWER FOR MY SOUL IN THE END!

YOU MUST LOOK AFTER YOUR OWN **SOUL**, YOU CAN'T LAY IT AT ANOTHER MAN'S DOOR LIKE AN **ORPHAN**.

IF YOU SUNDAY CABBIES WOULD **STRIKE**, RICH FOLK WOULD FIND ANOTHER WAY TO **CHURCH**, AND THAT'D BE THE **END** OF IT.

WHEN I WAS QUITE *TIRED*, I ATE GRASS IN THE WARM *SUNSHINE.*

JERRY HAD HIS LUNCH, AND PICKED *FLOWERS* FOR HIS LITTLE GIRL.

WE HAD A *GENTLE RIDE* HOME, WITH JERRY SINGING HAPPILY AS THE SUN SET.

WHEN JERRY HANDED DOLLY THE *FLOWERS*, SHE JUMPED FOR *JOY.* HE HAD NOT LOST HIS *SUNDAY* AFTER ALL.

CHAPTER 37: DOLLY AND A REAL GENTLEMAN

THAT *WINTER* WAS A LONG COLD ONE, WITH MUCH SLEET AND *SNOW*.

THE *CAB STAND* WAS NOT FAR FROM JERRY'S HOUSE, AND LITTLE DOLLY OFTEN BROUGHT HIM A POT OF *WARM SOUP*.

JERRY HAD BARELY *STARTED* HIS SOUP ONE DAY WHEN A GENTLEMAN *HAILED* US.

NO HURRY, LAD, *FINISH* YOUR SOUP FIRST.

THIS *KIND GENTLEMAN* BECAME A REGULAR CUSTOMER. HE LOVED ANIMALS, HAVING *THREE HAPPY DOGS* AT HOME. HE ALWAYS GAVE ME A SOFT WORD.

ONE DAY WE SAW HIM *SHOUT* AT A DRIVER WHO WAS *BEATING* HIS TEAM. HE TOOK DOWN THE MAN'S NAME TO *REPORT* HIM.

THIS WORLD WOULD BE A *BETTER PLACE* IF ONLY EVERYONE WOULD STAND BY THE OPPRESSED, AND *SPEAK OUT* AGAINST THE *WICKED.*

I WISH THERE WERE *MORE* LIKE YOU, SIR.

I SAY THAT IF WE SEE WRONGS AND DO *NOTHING,* WE ARE JUST AS *GUILTY* AS THE WRONG-DOERS!

CHAPTER 39: SEEDY SAM

ONE DAY A CABBY CALLED **SEEDY SAM** BROUGHT HIS HORSE IN.

YOUR HORSE LOOKS ALL **DONE IN**, SAM.

IF I COULD MAKE A **DECENT WAGE** I WOULDN'T HAVE TO MAKE HIM WORK SO **HARD**, GOV'NOR. AS IT IS, I BARELY MAKE A LIVING OUT OF HIM.

YOU THAT OWNS YOUR **RIGS** DO OK, BUT I HAVE TO **RENT** MINE, AND THAT'S A LOT OF **OVERHEAD**. I CANNOT RECALL THE LAST SUNDAY I HAD OFF, AND STILL I HARDLY GET BY.

I NEED A **NEW COAT**, BUT I CAN'T AFFORD THAT, NOT WITH **SIX MOUTHS** TO FEED. IT IS A DESPERATE **HARD LIFE**, AND IF A MAN SOMETIMES MISTREATS HIS ANIMAL, IS IT ANY WONDER?

100

EVERY WORD IS *TRUE*, SAM, YOU'LL GET NO ARGUMENT FROM ME. ALL I ASK IS THAT YOU GIVE YOUR HORSE A *KIND WORD* NOW AND THEN, IT'S AMAZING WHAT THEY *UNDERSTAND.*

I'LL SURELY *THINK* ON IT, GOV'NOR. <KAFF KAFF!>

SAM WAS NOT *SEEN* AT THE STAND FOR SEVERAL DAYS, THEN CAME THE *NEWS.*

GOV'NOR! SEEDY SAM IS *GONE!*

GONE? GOOD GOD, YOU MEAN *DEAD?*

AYE, HE TOOK A *FEVER* AND WENT QUICK. HIS *LAST WORDS* WERE, "I NEVER HAD A SUNDAY'S REST!"

LORD HA' *MERCY* ON US, BOYS, THIS IS A *WARNING* TO US ALL!

CHAPTER 40: POOR GINGER

ONE WINDY AFTERNOON A **SHABBY CAB** DREW UP NEXT TO US, PULLED BY A WORN OUT **CHESTNUT MARE.**

THE **POOR CREATURE** RAISED HER WEARY HEAD AND SAID:

"**BLACK BEAUTY!** IS THAT **YOU?**"

IT WAS **GINGER!**

SHE WAS SO **CHANGED** I HAD NOT RECOGNIZED HER. SHE HAD A **SORRY TALE** TO TELL.

"OH, BEAUTY," SHE SAID, "MY BREATH **NEVER RETURNED**, AND I HAVE BEEN SOLD AND **RESOLD**, UNTIL I HAVE COME TO THIS SORRY STATE.

"I CAN FIGHT NO LONGER, MEN ARE TOO STRONG AND **CRUEL**. I WISH I WAS DEAD, TO BE FREE OF THIS **MISERY!**"

TOO SOON HER DRIVER TOOK HER **AWAY**, LEAVING ME **SAD** AND MUCH TROUBLED.

CHAPTER 41: THE BUTCHER

ONE DAY WHEN WE HAD TO WAIT OUTSIDE A BUTCHER'S SHOP, THE *BUTCHER'S WAGON* PULLED UP WITH THE HORSE LOOKING NEARLY EXHAUSTED.

THE *BUTCHER* LIT INTO THE LAD WHO HAD DRIVEN THE WAGON.

WHAT DID I TELL YOU ABOUT *DRIVING* THE HORSE TO DEATH?! IF YOU WEREN'T MY OWN SON, I'D *FIRE* YOU ON THE SPOT!

IT'S NOT MY *FAULT*, YOU ALWAYS SAY, "NOW BE *QUICK!*" AND THE CUSTOMERS ARE ALWAYS IN A *HURRY!*

YES, YES, I KNOW IT TOO WELL! BUT WHO CARES FOR A BUTCHER'S *PROBLEMS*, OR A BUTCHERS HORSE?

NOW PUT HIM AWAY, AND GIVE HIM *EXTRA FEED* FOR HIS LABORS.

BUT NOT ALL BOYS ARE SO **HARD** ON THEIR CHARGES. THERE WAS A YOUNG LAD WHO DROVE A **VEGETABLE CART** WHO WAS BEST FRIENDS WITH HIS PONY.

THEY WERE SO **FOND** OF EACH OTHER IT WAS A TREAT TO SEE THEM TOGETHER. JERRY CALLED HIM **PRINCE CHARLIE**, FOR HE SAID HE WOULD BE THE KING OF DRIVERS ONE DAY.

THERE WAS AN OLD MAN WHO DROVE A *COAL CART* WHO WAS ALSO VERY CLOSE TO HIS *OLD HORSE*.

THEY USED TO *PLOD* ALONG LIKE TWO OLD PARTNERS, THE HORSE STOPPING OF HIS OWN ACCORD AT THE DOORS OF THEIR *REGULAR CUSTOMERS*.

JERRY SAID IT WAS A *COMFORT* TO THINK HOW HAPPY AN OLD HORSE COULD BE IN SUCH A POOR PLACE.

CHAPTER 42: THE ELECTION

JERRY, **MR. BALDWIN** WAS ASKING ABOUT YOUR VOTE. AND HE WANTS TO HIRE YOUR CAB FOR THE **ELECTION**.

POLLY MET US ONE DAY AFTER WORK IN SOME **DISTRESS**.

NO, I SHAN'T DO IT. IT WOULD BE AN **INSULT** TO THE HORSES. AS IF MY VOTE WERE HIS BUSINESS!

THE MORNING BEFORE THE **ELECTION**, LITTLE DOLLY BURST INTO THE YARD **SOBBING**, SPLATTERED WITH MUD.

DOLLY! WHATEVER HAS HAPPENED?

THOSE **NAUGHTY BOYS** HAVE THROWN **D-DIRT** ON ME FATHER, BECAUSE, B-BECAUSE... <SOB>

CHAPTER 43: A FRIEND IN NEED

AT LAST *ELECTION DAY* CAME, AND THERE WAS NO LACK OF *WORK* FOR JERRY AND I. IT WAS QUITE A HECTIC AFFAIR.

VOTE BLUE PARTY

VOTE RED

VOTE FOR

WE HAD JUST SETTLED IN FOR A QUICK BITE WHEN A YOUNG WOMAN CARRYING A *SICK CHILD* APPROACHED US.

PLEASE, SIR, CAN YOU TELL ME THE WAY...

...TO *ST. THOMAS'S HOSPITAL?*

WHY, MISSUS, IT'S *MILES AWAY!* LET ME TAKE YOU THERE.

THANK YOU, SIR, BUT I HAVE *NO MONEY!*

HEAVEN **BLESS YOU**, SIR!

I HAVE CHILDREN OF MY OWN, AND I'D BE **ASHAMED** TO MAKE YOU WALK ALL THAT WAY!

JUST THEN TWO **WELL-DRESSED MEN** RAN UP AND SPRANG INTO OUR CAB.

I'M SORRY, GENTLEMEN, THIS CAB IS **ENGAGED**.

BAH! SHE CAN WAIT! THIS IS **IMPORTANT**!

VERY WELL, GENTLEMEN, WE'LL HAVE A **CHAT** WHILE YOU REST YOURSELVES.

WHY, YOU **INSOLENT...!**

DON'T BOTHER, HERE'S **ANOTHER!**

ONE AFTERNOON JERRY AND CAPTAIN WERE RETURNING FROM LONDON BRIDGE WHEN THERE WAS A *TERRIBLE ACCIDENT.*

A *BEER WAGON* APPEARED AS IF FROM NOWHERE, IT'S DRIVER *WHIPPING* HIS TEAM UP TO FULL SPEED.

THEY *SMASHED* RIGHT INTO JERRY AND CAPTAIN!

JERRY WAS ONLY *BRUISED*, BUT CAPTAIN WAS VERY BADLY *HURT*.

THE WAGON DRIVER HAD BEEN *DRUNK*, AND WAS FINED, BUT NO AMOUNT OF MONEY COULD *HEAL* POOR CAPTAIN.

HE'LL NEVER BE RIGHT AGAIN, *POOR FELLOW*, SO WHAT AM I TO DO WITH HIM? CURSE ALL DRUNKS TO THE *PIT*, I SAY!

THE BOTTLE IS TOO GOOD A FRIEND FOR ME TO JOIN YOU IN THAT *CURSE*, I FEAR.

I MYSELF WAS ONCE **TOO FRIENDLY** WITH DRINK, GOVERNOR, BUT I KICKED IT, AND SO COULD **YOU.**

ONCE YOU ASK YOURSELF, "GIVE UP THE **BOTTLE** OR LOSE MY SOUL?" YOU ARE ON THE WAY TO BREAKING THE **CHAINS.**

I'VE A GREAT MIND TO **TRY** IT, FOR 'TIS A **POOR THING** NOT TO BE ONE'S OWN MASTER.

WE HAVE TO FACE MANY **HARD THINGS** IN THIS LIFE, GOVERNOR, AND IT IS BEST TO DO IT WITH A **CLEAR HEAD.**

OLD CAPTAIN IS LIKE A **DEAR FRIEND** TO ME, BUT THE ONLY THING I CAN SEE TO DO IS END HIS **SUFFERING** ONCE AND FOR ALL.

THE NEXT DAY HARRY TOOK ME TO THE **SMITH** FOR NEW SHOES.

WHEN I RETURNED, CAPTAIN WAS **GONE.**

117

JERRY NOW HAD TO FIND A **NEW HORSE.** HE HEARD OF ONE FOR SALE AT A **NOBLEMAN'S STABLE.** HE WAS A YOUNG HORSE NAMED **HOTSPUR.**

HE HAD **THROWN** HIS MASTER, WHO THEN ORDERED HIM TO BE SOLD. HIS GROOM CONFIDED THAT IT WAS **BAD RIDING** RATHER THAN A BAD HORSE THAT HAD GOTTEN HIS MASTER THROWN.

JERRY'S OWN **HORSE SENSE** TOLD HIM THIS WAS MOST LIKELY TRUE, SO A DEAL WAS MADE.

HOTSPUR AT FIRST THOUGHT HIS **NEW STATION** TO BE A GREAT COMEDOWN. BUT HE SOON **SETTLED IN,** AND WE ALL GOT ALONG VERY WELL.

CHAPTER 45: JERRY'S NEW YEAR

CHRISTMAS AND NEW YEAR'S ARE VERY *MERRY TIMES* FOR MOST, BUT FOR US THEY ARE *NO HOLIDAY*.

HAPPY PEOPLE *DANCE* AWAY WHILE WE STAND FOR HOURS IN THE *COLD* AND WET.

ON *NEW YEAR'S EVE* WE TOOK TWO GENTLEMEN TO A *CARD PARTY* AT NINE, AND WERE TOLD TO RETURN AT ELEVEN.

WE WERE AT THE DOOR AT ELEVEN, FOR JERRY WE ALWAYS *PROMPT*, BUT THE MEN WERE STILL INSIDE.

AT MIDNIGHT, THE RAIN HAD TURNED TO *SLEET*, AND STILL WE WAITED.

JERRY RANG THE *BELL*, AND WAS TOLD THE GENTLEMEN WOULD BE DOWN SOON.

JERRY BEGAN TO *COUGH*, A DEEP HACKING IN HIS CHEST THAT DID NOT BODE WELL.

AT A *QUARTER PAST ONE*, THE MEN EMERGED AT LAST. THEY GOT INTO THE CAB WITHOUT A WORD OF *THANKS*.

THEY *NEVER APOLOGIZED* FOR THE WAIT, BUT INSTEAD *COMPLAINED* ABOUT THE FARE.

WHEN AT LAST WE REACHED **HOME**, JERRY WAS COUGHING DREADFULLY.

OH DEAR, CAN'T I DO **SOMETHING**?

GET JACK SOMETHING **WARM**. THEN BOIL ME SOME **GRUEL**, PLEASE. <HACK HACK>

ALTHOUGH HE WAS NOW HACKING CONSTANTLY, JERRY **GROOMED** ME PROPERLY AND EVEN GAVE ME SOME **EXTRA HAY**. THEN HE STUMBLED INTO THE HOUSE.

IT WAS LATE THE **NEXT MORNING** BEFORE HARRY CAME TO **FEED** US. HE NEITHER WHISTLED OR SANG, BUT INSTEAD SPOKE TO US IN A **SMALL, QUIET VOICE.**

HE TOLD US THAT JERRY WAS **DANGEROUSLY ILL**, AND THAT THE DOCTOR HAD COME, AND SAID THAT HE MIGHT EVEN DIE.

DOLLY CAME WITH HARRY THE *NEXT DAY*, AND PETTING US QUIETLY, SHE SAID, "HE'S *NO* BETTER, MY PRETTIES, NO BETTER AT ALL."

ON THE *THIRD DAY*, GOVERNOR GRANT CAME INTO THE STABLE.

HARRY, MY BOY, HOW IS YOUR *FATHER?*

VERY BAD, SIR.

THE DOCTOR IS NOT SURE HE'LL MAKE IT.

SOUNDS BAD INDEED, BUT WHILST THERE'S LIFE THERE'S *HOPE*, AS THEY SAY.

YES, THE DOCTOR SAID THAT HE HAS A *BETTER CHANCE* THAN MOST, AS HE DOES NOT DRINK.

IF THERE'S ANY RULE THAT *GOOD MEN* SHOULD GET OVER THESE THINGS, I'M SURE THAT HE WILL, MY BOY, HE'S THE *BEST MAN* I KNOW.

JERRY MADE IT THROUGH THE NIGHT, AND IN THE MORNING HIS *FEVER* HAD BROKEN.

IT WAS QUICKLY SETTLED THAT AS SOON AS JERRY WAS WELL ENOUGH, THEY SHOULD MOVE TO THE COUNTRY. THE CAB AND HORSES WOULD BE *SOLD* AS SOON AS POSSIBLE.

POLLY AND THE CHILDREN CAME TO BID ME A *TEARFUL FAREWELL.* JERRY WAS STILL *TOO WEAK* TO LEAVE HIS BED, AND SO I NEVER SAW HIM AGAIN.

R 47: HARD TIMES

N HAD CAUSE TO
TION JUST HOW
HAD BEEN, FOR I
D TO THE VERY CAB
THAT HAD WORKED
GINGER TO DEATH.

CH AS I HAD SEEN
IT WAS NOT UNTIL
HAT I KNEW THE
MISERY OF A CAB
RSES' LIFE.

I WAS WORKED SEVEN DAYS A WEEK AND *WHIPPED* SO CRUELLY AT EVERY TURN THAT I WISHED I MIGHT, LIKE GINGER, DROP *DEAD*.

ONE DAY MY *WISH* VERY NEARLY CAME TO PASS.

IS THIS WAGON NOT *OVERLOADED*, SIR?

YES, YES, THE FOREMAN *ORDERED* IT, BUT WHAT CAN I DO ABOUT THAT?

HE CANNOT USE ALL HIS *POWER* WITH HIS HEAD HELD *BACK* WITH THAT BEARING REIN. I YOU WOULD TAKE IT *OFF*, I AM SURE HE WOULD DO BETTER!

OH, VERY WELL, *ANYTHING* TO PLEASE A *LADY*.

POOR FELLOW! LET ME TAKE THIS OFF. ISN'T THAT MUCH BETTER?

WHAT A *COMFORT* IT WAS! NOW I FELT *READY* FOR ANYTHING!

JAKES GOT DOWN AND TOOK THE *REINS*, AND I GAVE IT MY ALL. WE WERE SOON AT THE *TOP* OF THE HILL.

I SAY, THAT WAS A *REAL LADY!* I WILL TRY HER PLAN, *UPHILL*, AT ANY RATE.

TO HIS CREDIT, JAKES KEPT HIS *WORD*, BUT MY *LOADS* DID NOT GET ANY LIGHTER.

YOU SEE, HE WAS QUITE *WILLING* WHEN YOU GAVE HIM THE *CHANCE*. YOU WON'T PUT THAT REIN ON AGAIN, WILL YOU?

AYE, I CAN'T DENY IT, BUT I'D BE A *LAUGHING STOCK* IF I LEFT 'EM OFF, IT'S THE FASHION, YOU SEE.

IS IT NOT BETTER TO LEAD A *GOOD FASHION* THAN TO FOLLOW A BAD ONE? PLEASE *THINK* ON IT, SIR. GOOD DAY TO YOU NOW.

MY *STRENGTH* SOON BEGAN TO *FAIL* ME, AND I WAS TAKEN OFF THE WAGONS FOR SOME REST.

I THOUGHT MYSELF *LUCKY* THAT I WAS SOLD BEFORE I WENT *BLIND*.

CHAPT

I SO
QUE
LUCKY
WAS SO
COMPAN
POOR

AS M
BEFOR
NOW
LITTER
H

THE SAME MAN KEPT *PETTING* ME AND *ENCOURAGING* ME UNTIL I FELT STRONG ENOUGH TO *STAGGER* TO MY FEET.

THIS KIND *STRANGER* LED ME SLOWLY BACK TO THE CAB COMPANY STABLES.

THE NEXT MORNING THE **OWNER** OF THE CAB COMPANY CAME WITH A **FARRIER** TO LOOK ME OVER.

THIS IS A CASE OF **OVERWORK** MORE THAN DISEASE. IF YOU COULD GIVE HIM **SIX MONTHS** OFF, HE WOULD BE ABLE TO WORK AGAIN.

MY **PLAN** IS TO WORK 'EM AS LONG AS THEY'LL GO, THEN **SELL** 'EM.

WELL, THERE'S A **SALE** IN TEN DAYS. IF YOU **REST** HIM AND FEED HIM UP, HE MAY **RECOVER** ENOUGH TO SELL THERE.

THE OWNER RATHER UNWILLINGLY **AGREED,** AND FOR TEN DAYS I WAS WELL CARED FOR.

I LOOKED FORWARD TO THE SALE, THINKING THAT ANY **CHANGE** WOULD BE FOR THE BETTER.

136

CHAPTER 48: FARMER THOROUGHGOOD AND HIS GRANDSON WILLIE

SO IT WAS THAT I ONCE AGAIN FOUND MYSELF AT A *HORSE FAIR*.

AT THIS SALE, I FOUND MYSELF IN COMPANY WITH THE OLD BROKEN-DOWN HORSES.

MOST OF THE MEN HERE LOOKED AS BROKEN-DOWN AS THE HORSES, EXCEPT FOR ONE *OLD MAN* AND HIS GRANDSON.

WHAT DO YOU THINK OF *THIS ONE*, GRANDPA?

HE HAS SEEN *BETTER DAYS*, BUT THERE IS SOME *BREEDING* IN HIM, PROBABLY PULLED A FANCY CARRIAGE ONCE, HMM

THE OLD MAN WENT OVER ME *EXPERTLY* AS THE DEALER TOLD MY TALE.

HE'S *WORN DOWN* FROM CAB WORK, BUT SOME *GOOD REST* WOULD SET HIM RIGHT AS RAIN.

HE WOULD DO WELL IN OUR *MEADOW*, GRANDPA.

I TRIED TO LOOK MY *BEST* AS THE DEALER TROTTED ME OUT.

VERY WELL! 'TIS A *SPECULATION*, BUT WORTH IT, I THINK.

YOU'LL NOT *REGRET* IT, SIR.

THANK YOU, GRANDPA!

SO I WAS TURNED OUT INTO THE *FINE MEADOW* OF FARMER THOROUGHGOOD, WHO GAVE ORDERS THAT I BE *FATTENED UP* WITH GOOD HAY AND OATS.

HIS GRANDSON, WILLIE, TOOK CHARGE OF MY *RECOVERY*, AND MADE A GOOD JOB OF IT.

HE VISITED ME EVERY DAY WITH A *KIND WORD* AND A BIT OF CARROT, AND I GREW VERY *FOND* OF HIM.

FARMER THOROUGHGOOD WOULD GO OVER ME FROM TIME TO TIME, AND SEEMED *PLEASED* WITH MY PROGRESS.

HE IS LOOKING OH SO MUCH *BETTER*, GRANDPA!

AYE, M'BOY, YOU MADE A *GOOD CHOICE* WITH THIS ONE. I BELIEVE WE WILL SEE A *CHANGE* FOR THE BETTER IN THE *SPRING*.

ALL THIS *GOOD CARE* HAD INDEED IMPROVED MY CONDITION AS WELL AS MY *SPIRITS*. DURING THE LONG WINTER, I BEGAN TO FEEL QUITE WELL AGAIN.

WHEN **SPRING** FINALLY CAME ROUND, I WAS HITCHED TO A **SMALL CARRIAGE** AND PUT THROUGH MY **PACES.** IT WAS GOOD TO WORK, AND I FELT LIKE MYSELF AGAIN.

HE HAS GROWN **YOUNG** IN YOUR CARE, WILLIE. HE OWES YOU HIS LIFE.

HOW **GLAD** I AM YOU BOUGHT HIM! NOW WE MUST FIND A **GOOD HOME** FOR HIM.

CHAPTER 49: MY LAST HOME

BY THE SUMMER, I HAD COME TO UNDERSTAND THAT THIS WAS THE **BUSINESS** OF FARMER THOROUGHGOOD, TO **SAVE** WORN DOWN HORSES, AND FIND **GOOD HOMES** FOR THEM.

WE HAVE DONE **ALL** WE CAN FOR YOU, **MY FRIEND**. NOW IT IS TIME TO SAY GOOD BYE.

WE WENT TO THE HOME OF **THREE LADIES** THAT FARMER THOROUGHGOOD KNEW, WHO WERE IN NEED OF A HORSE.

THE THREE LOOKED ME OVER, AND DECIDED TO TRY ME ON A **TRIAL BASIS.** THEIR GROOM WOULD PICK ME UP IN THE MORNING.

YOU'LL MAKE A **FINE MATCH**, LADIES, I GUARANTEE IT!

WHEN THE GROOM ARRIVED, HE LOOKED SHARPLY AT MY **SCARRED KNEES.**

I AM SURPRISED, SIR, THAT YOU'D RECOMMEND SUCH A **BLEMISHED HORSE** TO MY LADIES.

HANDSOME IS AS **HANDSOME DOES,** YOUNG MAN. YOU WILL FIND NO OTHER **FAULTS** IN THIS HORSE, BELIEVE ME!

BACK AT THE LADIES STABLE, THE GROOM WAS **CLEANING** ME WHEN HE **STOPPED** AT AN OLD SCAR.

HMM, I KNEW A **HORSE** WITH A SCAR LIKE THIS, HE LOOKED MUCH LIKE YOU, HIS NAME WAS **BLACK BEAUTY.**

I STARTED ON HEARING MY **OLD NAME.** WHO WAS THIS GROOM?

BLACK BEAUTY! IT IS **YOU!** I AM LITTLE **JOE GREEN,** FROM SQUIRE GORDON'S STABLES!

LATER, JOE HITCHED ME TO A **SMALL CARRIAGE,** AND ONE OF THE LADIES GAVE ME A **TRY.** JOE TOLD HER I WAS THE BLACK BEAUTY HE HAD KNOWN AS A CHILD.

WHEN WE RETURNED, SHE TOLD **JOE'S STORY** TO THE LADIES. ONE OF THEM EXCLAIMED:

BLACK BEAUTY! I SHALL WRITE TO MY **FRIEND** MRS. GORDON, AND TELL HER THAT HER **FAVORITE HORSE** HAS COME TO US. HOW **PLEASED** SHE WILL BE!

AFTER THIS, IT WAS QUITE DECIDED TO **KEEP** ME, AND CALL ME BY MY **OLD NAME.**

WILLIE COMES TO **VISIT** ME WHEN HE CAN, AND WE ARE STILL **SPECIAL FRIENDS.**

MY LADIES HAVE PROMISED **NEVER** TO SELL ME, AND SO MY **TROUBLES** ARE OVER.

THIS IS A **GOOD HOME**, AND I HAVE NOTHING TO FEAR.

AND OFTEN BEFORE I AM QUITE AWAKE, I FANCY I AM STILL IN THE **ORCHARD** AT BIRTWICK, STANDING WITH MY **OLD FRIENDS** UNDER THE APPLE TREES.

THE END